George Mason Library
2601 Cameron Mills Rd.
Alexandria, Virginia 22302

WELCOME TO THE U.S.A.
ARKANSAS

Written by Ann Heinrichs   Illustrated by Matt Kania
Content Adviser: Michael B. Dougan, PhD, Professor of History,
Arkansas State University, Jonesboro, Arkansas

The Child's World

Published in the United States of America by The Child's World®
PO Box 326 • Chanhassen, MN 55317-0326
800-599-READ • www.childsworld.com

Photo Credits
Cover: Bernie Jungkind/CJRW/Arkansas Parks & Tourism; frontispiece:
Arkansas Parks & Tourism.

Interior: AP/Wide World Photo: 30 (Spencer Tirey), 33 (Danny Johnston);
Arkansas Parks & Tourism: 6, 14, 18, 21, 22, 25, 26, 29, 34; Conway Area
Chamber of Commerce: 13; Corbis: 9 (Buddy Mays), 10 (Bob Krist), 17
(Tim Thompson).

Acknowledgments
The Child's World®: Mary Berendes, Publishing Director

Editorial Directions, Inc.: E. Russell Primm, Editorial Director; Katie Marsico, Associate
Editor; Judith Shiffer, Assistant Editor; Matt Messbarger, Editorial Assistant; Susan
Hindman, Copy Editor; Melissa McDaniel, Proofreader; Kevin Cunningham, Peter
Garnham, Matt Messbarger, Olivia Nellums, Chris Simms, Molly Symmonds, Katherine
Trickle, Carl Stephen Wender, Fact Checkers; Tim Griffin/IndexServ, Indexer; Cian
Loughlin O'Day, Photo Researcher and Editor

The Design Lab: Kathleen Petelinsek, Design and art production

Copyright © 2006 by The Child's World®
All rights reserved. No part of this book may be reproduced or utilized in any form or by
any means without written permission from the publisher.

Library of Congress Cataloging-in-Publication Data
Heinrichs, Ann.
  Arkansas / by Ann Heinrichs ; cartography and illustrations by Matt Kania.
    p. cm. — (Welcome to the U.S.A.)
  Includes index.
  ISBN 1-59296-469-9 (library bound : alk. paper)
  1. Arkansas—Juvenile literature. I. Kania, Matt. II. Title.
  F411.3.H454 2005
  976.7—dc22   2005013211

Ann Heinrichs is the author of more than 100 books for children and young adults. She has also enjoyed successful careers as a children's book editor and an advertising copywriter. Ann grew up in Fort Smith, Arkansas, and lives in Chicago, Illinois.

About the Author
Ann Heinrichs

Matt Kania loves maps and, as a kid, dreamed of making them. In school he studied geography and cartography, and today he makes maps for a living. Matt's favorite thing about drawing maps is learning about the places they represent. Many of the maps he has created can be found in books, magazines, videos, Web sites, and public places.

About the
Map Illustrator
Matt Kania

On the cover: Want an amazing view of the Ozarks? Hike out to Whitaker Point!
On page one: Boom! Join the festivities in Little Rock's River Market District.

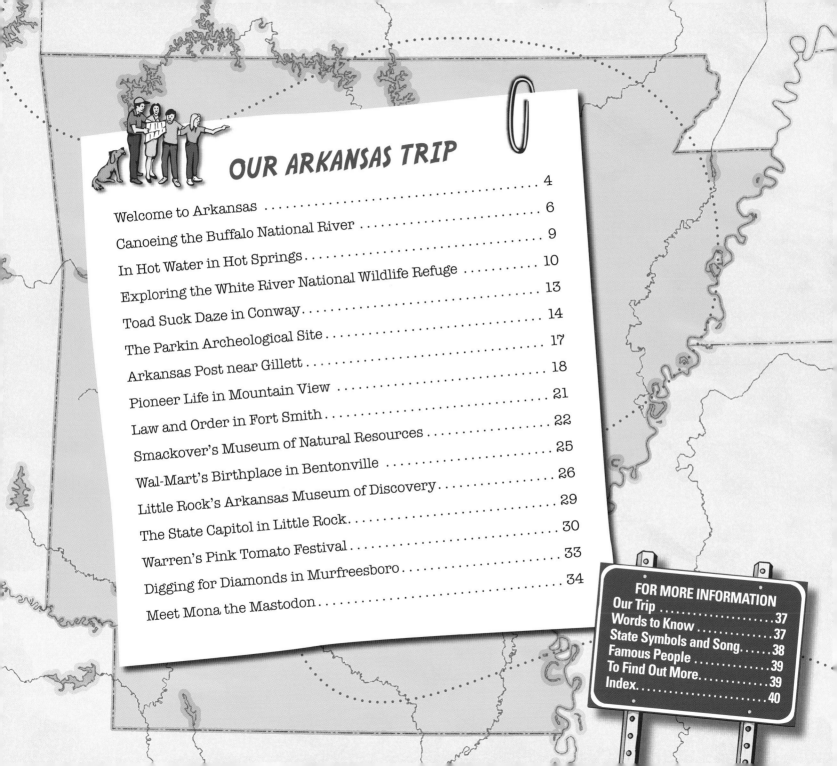

OUR ARKANSAS TRIP

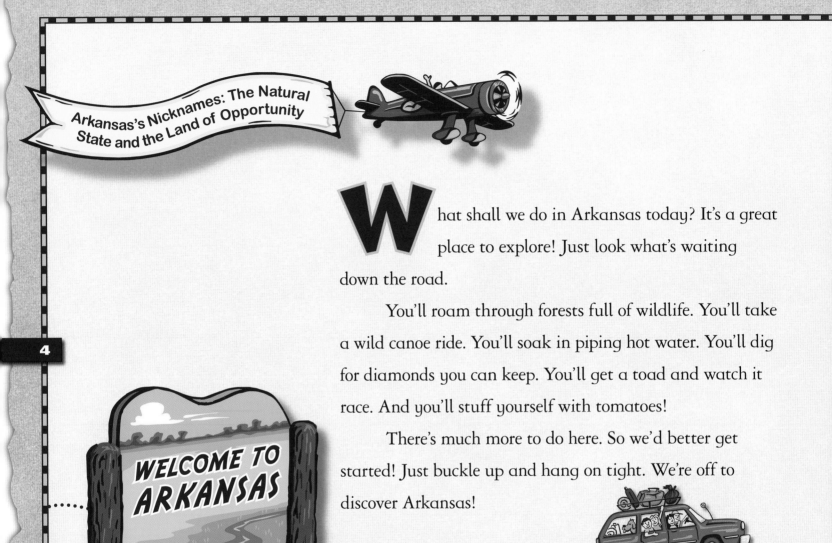

What shall we do in Arkansas today? It's a great place to explore! Just look what's waiting down the road.

You'll roam through forests full of wildlife. You'll take a wild canoe ride. You'll soak in piping hot water. You'll dig for diamonds you can keep. You'll get a toad and watch it race. And you'll stuff yourself with tomatoes!

There's much more to do here. So we'd better get started! Just buckle up and hang on tight. We're off to discover Arkansas!

WELCOME TO ARKANSAS

As you travel through Arkansas, watch for all the interesting facts along the way.

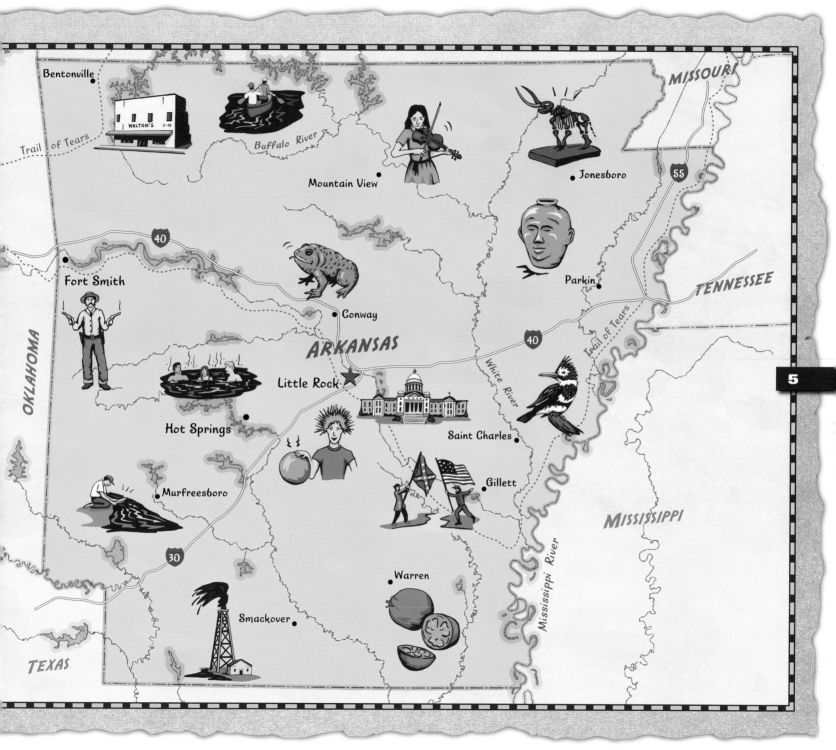

Bentonville

Trail of Tears

WALTON'S 5-10

Buffalo River

Mountain View

Jonesboro

MISSOURI

55

Parkin

TENNESSEE

Fort Smith

40

Conway

ARKANSAS

40

White River

Trail of Tears

OKLAHOMA

Little Rock

Hot Springs

Saint Charles

Gillett

Murfreesboro

Warren

MISSISSIPPI

30

Smackover

Mississippi River

TEXAS

The Buffalo River looks pretty quiet. But watch out—there are rapids ahead!

The Buffalo River was the nation's 1st national river. Laws protect national rivers from dams and other construction. The Buffalo River rises near Boxley. Then it flows into the White River near Buffalo City.

Canoeing the Buffalo National River

Wahoo! What a wild ride! You'll love canoeing down the Buffalo National River. Some sections are smooth, but some are rough. Hang on tight!

This river winds through the Ozark Mountains. The Ozarks cover north and northwest Arkansas. They slope down toward the Arkansas River. This river flows southeast across the state. It empties into the great Mississippi River. The Ouachita Mountains reach into west-central Arkansas. Many lakes and streams sparkle among the mountains. Hot-water springs bubble up from underground, too. The Mississippi River forms Arkansas's eastern border. Land along the river is very fertile. It's often called the Mississippi Delta.

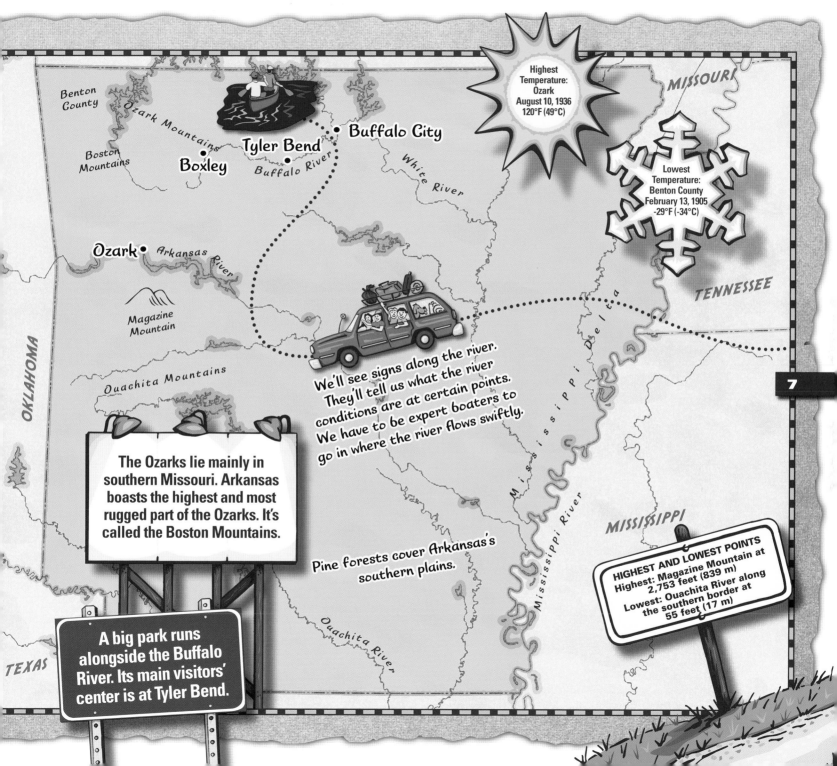

Benton County

Ozark Mountains

Boston Mountains

Boxley

Tyler Bend

Buffalo River

Buffalo City

White River

Highest Temperature: Ozark August 10, 1936 120°F (49°C)

Lowest Temperature: Benton County February 13, 1905 -29°F (-34°C)

MISSOURI

TENNESSEE

Ozark

Arkansas River

Magazine Mountain

Ouachita Mountains

OKLAHOMA

Mississippi Delta

Mississippi River

MISSISSIPPI

We'll see signs along the river. They'll tell us what the river conditions are at certain points. We have to be expert boaters to go in where the river flows swiftly.

Pine forests cover Arkansas's southern plains.

The Ozarks lie mainly in southern Missouri. Arkansas boasts the highest and most rugged part of the Ozarks. It's called the Boston Mountains.

Ouachita River

TEXAS

A big park runs alongside the Buffalo River. Its main visitors' center is at Tyler Bend.

HIGHEST AND LOWEST POINTS
Highest: Magazine Mountain at 2,753 feet (839 m)
Lowest: Ouachita River along the southern border at 55 feet (17 m)

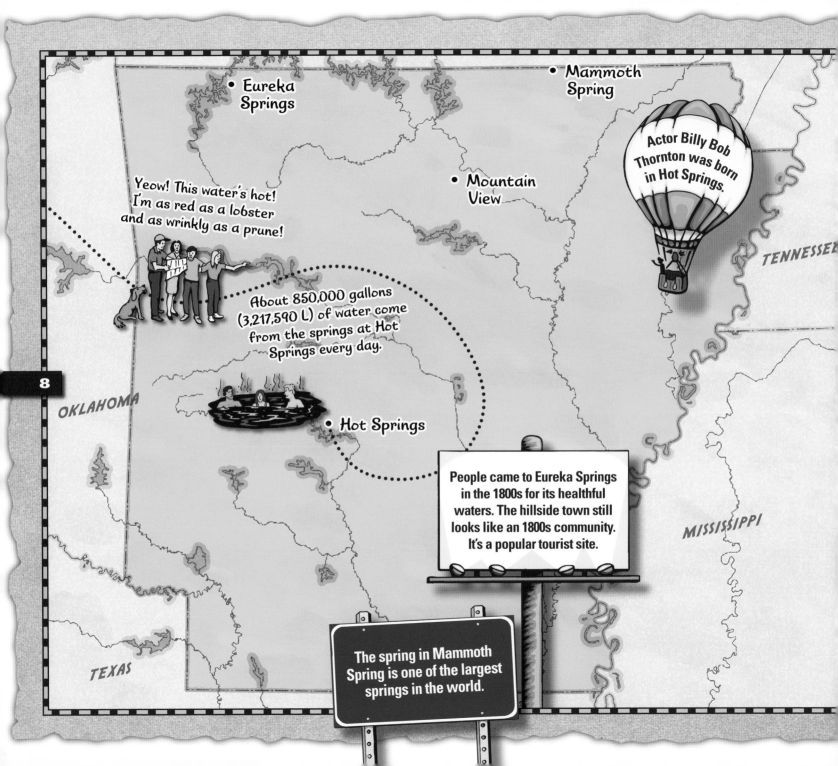

Eureka Springs

Mammoth Spring

Actor Billy Bob Thornton was born in Hot Springs.

Mountain View

Yeow! This water's hot! I'm as red as a lobster and as wrinkly as a prune!

About 850,000 gallons (3,217,590 L) of water come from the springs at Hot Springs every day.

Hot Springs

People came to Eureka Springs in the 1800s for its healthful waters. The hillside town still looks like an 1800s community. It's a popular tourist site.

The spring in Mammoth Spring is one of the largest springs in the world.

TENNESSEE

MISSISSIPPI

OKLAHOMA

TEXAS

In Hot Water in Hot Springs

Suppose you say you're in hot water. What does that mean? It means you're in big trouble! But not in Hot Springs. Here, it means you're taking a healthful bath!

Rich people and sick people once came here. They soaked in the waters to improve their health. The water gushes from forty-seven underground springs. It was pumped into buildings along **Bathhouse** Row.

Try a nice, hot soak. But there's much more to do around here. Hot Springs National Park covers a big area. Hike through its forested mountains. Just don't get too close to a steep mountainside. You'll be in hot water!

Tubs at the Fordyce Bathhouse didn't need heaters. The water from the springs was already hot!

Blanchard Springs Caverns is near Mountain View. This cave system has miles of underground passages. Its largest room is 4 football fields long!

Ducks and geese enjoy sunrise on the White River.

10

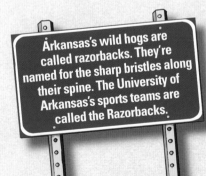

Arkansas's wild hogs are called razorbacks. They're named for the sharp bristles along their spine. The University of Arkansas's sports teams are called the Razorbacks.

Creep through the White River National Wildlife Refuge. You're bound to see lots of animals. When's the best time to look for them? In the early morning or late afternoon. Animals roam around when the sun's not too hot.

Look by the river or around a pond. Animals go there to drink. You'll see deer, beavers, foxes, and wild hogs. You might even spot alligators or bears. You'll see plenty of turtles, lizards, and frogs. Kingfishers fish by the water, and ducks swim past you. Eagles and hawks soar high above you. They're looking for small animals to eat!

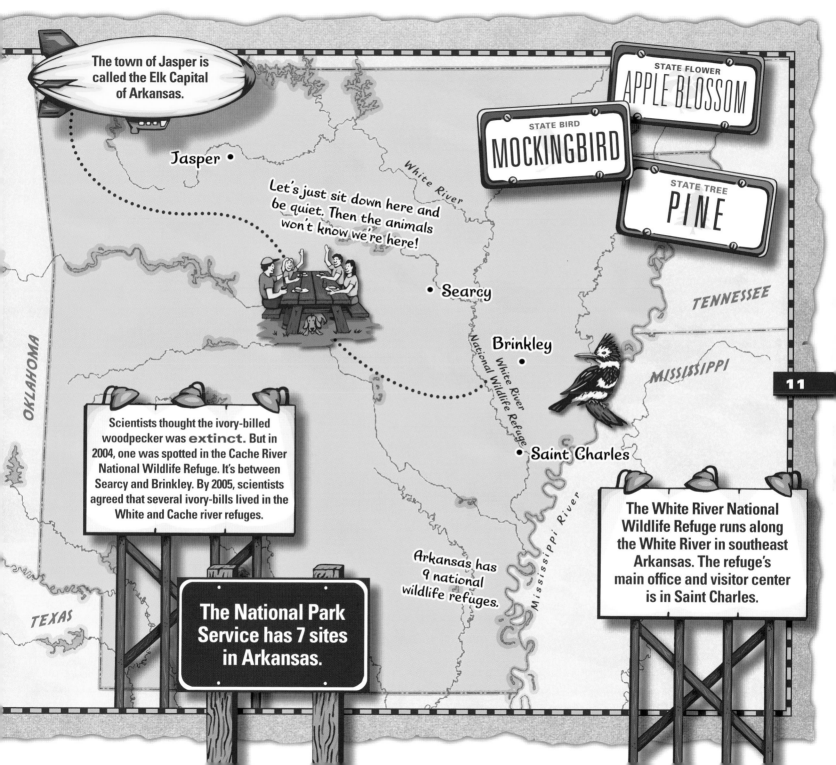

The town of Jasper is called the Elk Capital of Arkansas.

STATE FLOWER
APPLE BLOSSOM

STATE BIRD
MOCKINGBIRD

STATE TREE
PINE

Jasper •

Let's just sit down here and be quiet. Then the animals won't know we're here!

• Searcy

Brinkley •

• Saint Charles

Scientists thought the ivory-billed woodpecker was **extinct**. But in 2004, one was spotted in the Cache River National Wildlife Refuge. It's between Searcy and Brinkley. By 2005, scientists agreed that several ivory-bills lived in the White and Cache river refuges.

The White River National Wildlife Refuge runs along the White River in southeast Arkansas. The refuge's main office and visitor center is in Saint Charles.

Arkansas has 9 national wildlife refuges.

The National Park Service has 7 sites in Arkansas.

OKLAHOMA

TEXAS

TENNESSEE

MISSISSIPPI

White River

White River National Wildlife Refuge

Mississippi River

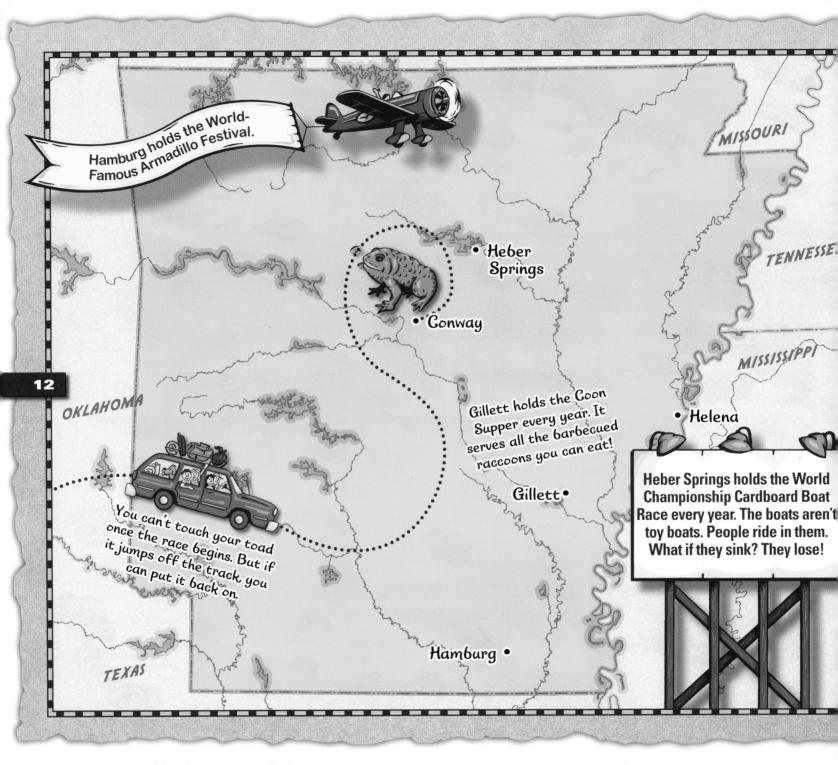

Hamburg holds the World-Famous Armadillo Festival.

MISSOURI

TENNESSE

MISSISSIPPI

Heber Springs

Conway

OKLAHOMA

Gillett holds the Coon Supper every year. It serves all the barbecued raccoons you can eat!

Helena

Gillett

Heber Springs holds the World Championship Cardboard Boat Race every year. The boats aren't toy boats. People ride in them. What if they sink? They lose!

You can't touch your toad once the race begins. But if it jumps off the track, you can put it back on.

Hamburg

TEXAS

Toad Suck Daze in Conway

Pick out a toad from the toad pen. Or bring your own toad if you like. Then line up for the Toad Jump race. It's time for Toad Suck Daze!

This is a really fun festival in Conway. It offers pony rides and a petting zoo. There's a Baby Crawl race. And there's the Tour de Toad bike race. But don't miss the Toad Jump race.

No frogs may enter—only toads. What's the difference? Toads have rough, dry, lumpy skin. But frogs have smooth, moist skin. Happy hopping!

Hey! It's not easy to get a toad to jump!

The King Biscuit Blues Festival is held in Helena every year. Its name comes from Helena's King Biscuit Time radio show.

Want to learn about the past? Just head to Parkin!

Hernando de Soto and his men traveled around Arkansas from 1541 to 1543. They may have introduced diseases that killed entire villages.

The Parkin Archeological Site

Who lived in Arkansas 1,000 years ago? Just visit Parkin, and you'll see. Native Americans lived there from about 1000 to 1550. A deep ditch surrounded their village for safety. They made pottery jugs molded to look like human faces. They grew corn, beans, and other crops.

Hernando de Soto arrived in Arkansas in 1541. He was a Spanish explorer. De Soto visited a village he called Casqui. **Historians** believe the Parkin site is that village.

You can visit Parkin **Archeological** State Park. You'll see the American Indians' art, pottery, and tools. And you'll watch scientists dig for ancient objects.

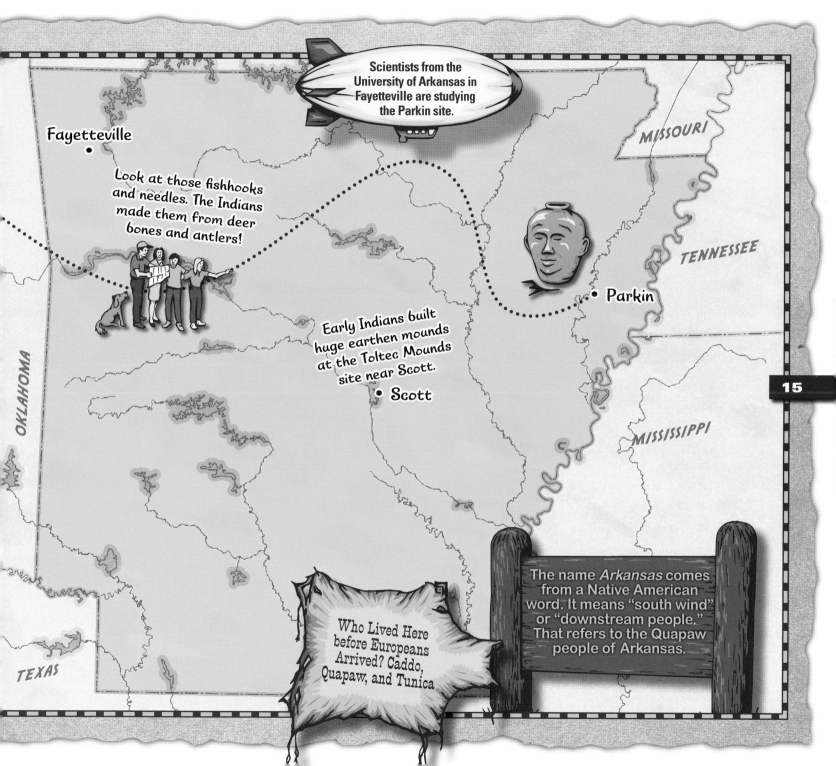

Scientists from the University of Arkansas in Fayetteville are studying the Parkin site.

MISSOURI

Fayetteville

Look at those fishhooks and needles. The Indians made them from deer bones and antlers!

TENNESSEE

• Parkin

OKLAHOMA

Early Indians built huge earthen mounds at the Toltec Mounds site near Scott.

• Scott

MISSISSIPPI

TEXAS

Who Lived Here before Europeans Arrived? Caddo, Quapaw, and Tunica

The name *Arkansas* comes from a Native American word. It means "south wind" or "downstream people." That refers to the Quapaw people of Arkansas.

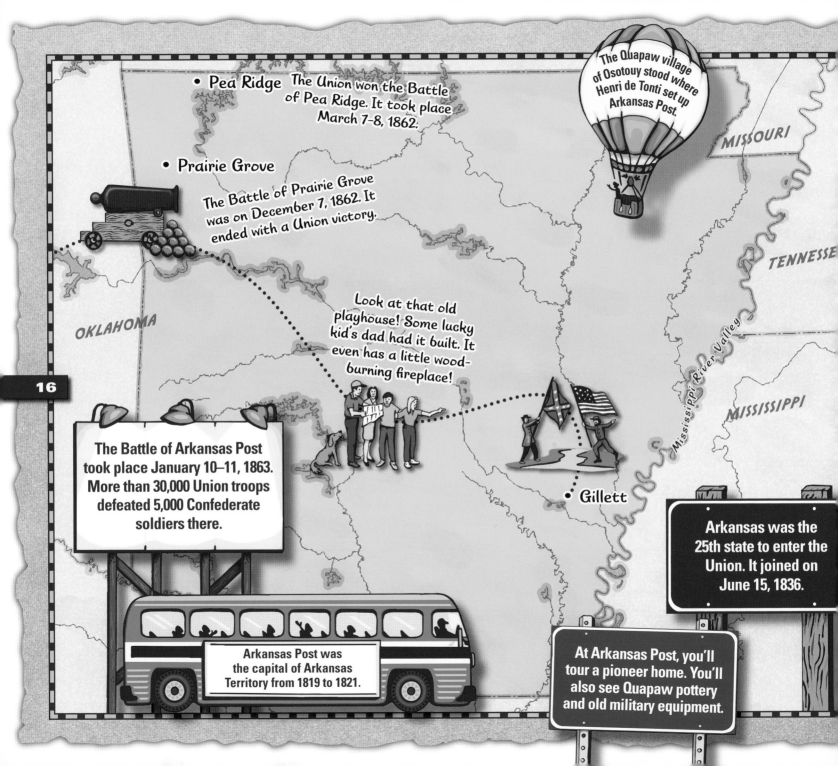

• Pea Ridge The Union won the Battle of Pea Ridge. It took place March 7-8, 1862.

• Prairie Grove

The Battle of Prairie Grove was on December 7, 1862. It ended with a Union victory.

The Quapaw village of Osotouy stood where Henri de Tonti set up Arkansas Post.

OKLAHOMA

Look at that old playhouse! Some lucky kid's dad had it built. It even has a little wood-burning fireplace!

MISSOURI

TENNESSEE

Mississippi River Valley

MISSISSIPPI

The Battle of Arkansas Post took place January 10–11, 1863. More than 30,000 Union troops defeated 5,000 Confederate soldiers there.

• Gillett

Arkansas Post was the capital of Arkansas Territory from 1819 to 1821.

Arkansas was the 25th state to enter the Union. It joined on June 15, 1836.

At Arkansas Post, you'll tour a pioneer home. You'll also see Quapaw pottery and old military equipment.

Want to walk through 300 years of history? Just stroll through Arkansas Post. It was Arkansas's first white settlement. Frenchman Henri de Tonti founded it in 1686.

France claimed present-day Arkansas at that time. The United States took over in 1803. Arkansas Territory was established in 1819. By then, Arkansas Post was a busy river port. It became the new territory's capital.

Arkansas Post was destroyed during the Civil War (1861–1865). Northern and Southern states were fighting over states' rights and slavery. Arkansas was on the Confederate side. Northern states formed the Union side. In the end, the Union won the war.

Hey! Where's the microwave? Learn about life for early settlers at Arkansas Post.

René-Robert Cavelier, Sieur de La Salle, claimed the Mississippi River valley for France in 1682. That included present-day Arkansas.

Is this a hoedown? Musicians perform at the Ozark Folk Center.

Folk singer and songwriter Jimmy Driftwood was born in Mountain View.

Suppose you lived way up in the mountains. How would you get soap, toys, or clothes? You'd make them!

That's what Arkansas **pioneers** did in the 1800s. They settled in the rugged mountains. They were far from towns or stores. Their skills helped them stay alive.

Mountain View preserves this way of life. Just visit the Ozark Folk Center. You'll see people making brooms, pottery, and soap. Some are making dolls, candles, or musical instruments. Fiddlers and banjo players strike up tunes. And everyone's happy to explain what they're doing. Do you wish you lived back in pioneer days?

18

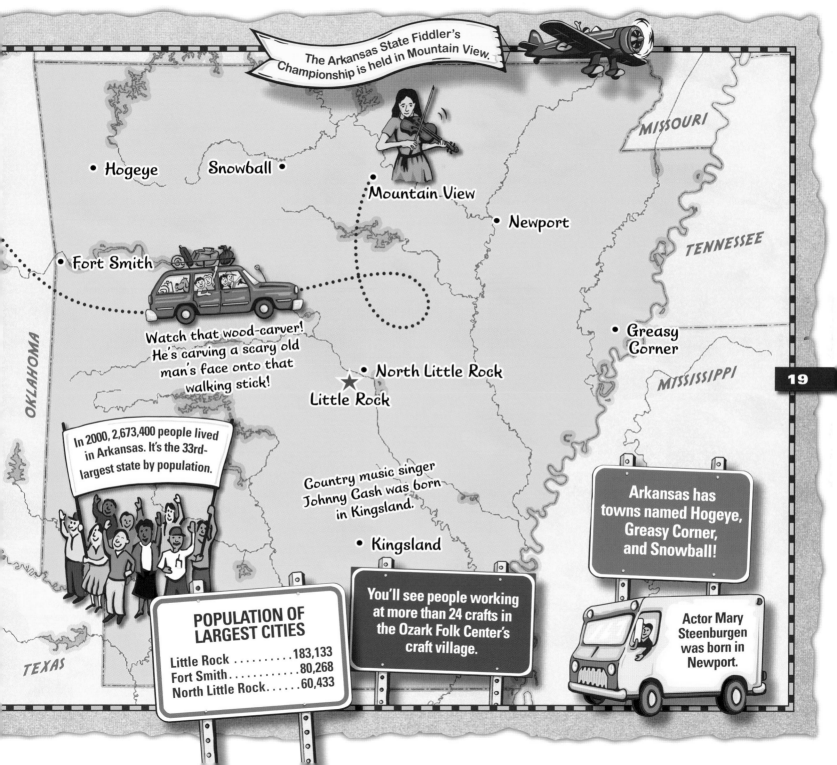

The Arkansas State Fiddler's Championship is held in Mountain View.

MISSOURI

- Hogeye   Snowball •

• Mountain View

• Newport

TENNESSEE

• Fort Smith

Watch that wood-carver! He's carving a scary old man's face onto that walking stick!

• Greasy Corner

MISSISSIPPI

19

OKLAHOMA

★ • North Little Rock
Little Rock

In 2000, 2,673,400 people lived in Arkansas. It's the 33rd-largest state by population.

Country music singer Johnny Cash was born in Kingsland.

Arkansas has towns named Hogeye, Greasy Corner, and Snowball!

• Kingsland

POPULATION OF LARGEST CITIES

Little Rock	183,133
Fort Smith	80,268
North Little Rock	60,433

You'll see people working at more than 24 crafts in the Ozark Folk Center's craft village.

Actor Mary Steenburgen was born in Newport.

TEXAS

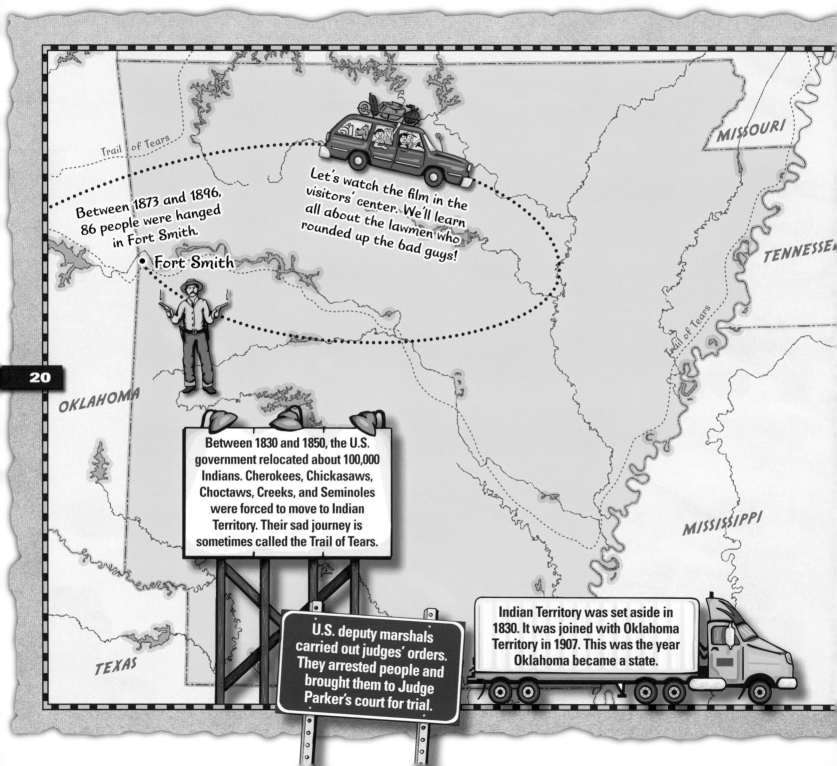

Trail of Tears

MISSOURI

TENNESSEE

Between 1873 and 1896, 86 people were hanged in Fort Smith.

Let's watch the film in the visitors' center. We'll learn all about the lawmen who rounded up the bad guys!

• Fort Smith

Trail of Tears

OKLAHOMA

Between 1830 and 1850, the U.S. government relocated about 100,000 Indians. Cherokees, Chickasaws, Choctaws, Creeks, and Seminoles were forced to move to Indian Territory. Their sad journey is sometimes called the Trail of Tears.

MISSISSIPPI

U.S. deputy marshals carried out judges' orders. They arrested people and brought them to Judge Parker's court for trial.

Indian Territory was set aside in 1830. It was joined with Oklahoma Territory in 1907. This was the year Oklahoma became a state.

TEXAS

Glance around the old courtroom. You can almost hear the judge's booming voice. Look at the old jail cells. Many outlaws spent their last days here. Then gaze at the **gallows.** That's where the outlaws were hanged.

You're touring the Fort Smith National Historic Site. Judge Isaac Parker ruled over the court here. He was known as the Hanging Judge.

Fort Smith is right on the Oklahoma border. In the 1800s, Oklahoma was Indian Territory. Outlaws roamed this wild, untamed land. But some got caught. Judge Parker's job was to decide their fate.

Guilty or innocent? Judge Parker decided people's fate at Fort Smith.

21

Judge Parker was the federal judge for the Western District of Arkansas. He was also the judge for Indian Territory. He held this post from 1875 to 1896.

Look! A street with early 1900s cars in the Arkansas Museum of Natural Resources.

Smackover's Museum of Natural Resources

Today, it's easy to get gasoline for cars. We just drive to a gas station. But things were different in the 1920s. Cars were a fairly new invention. And the oil **industry** was new, too. (Petroleum, or oil, is made into gasoline.)

You'll learn about these days in Smackover. Just visit the Arkansas Museum of Natural Resources! Outdoors, you'll see working oil **derricks.** Indoors, you'll see old cars and gas-station pumps.

Oil was discovered in El Dorado in 1921. Smackover's first oil well opened in 1922. Thousands of people swarmed in to get jobs. It was an exciting time!

About 100 people lived in Smackover before oil was found there. The population quickly swelled to 20,000 people.

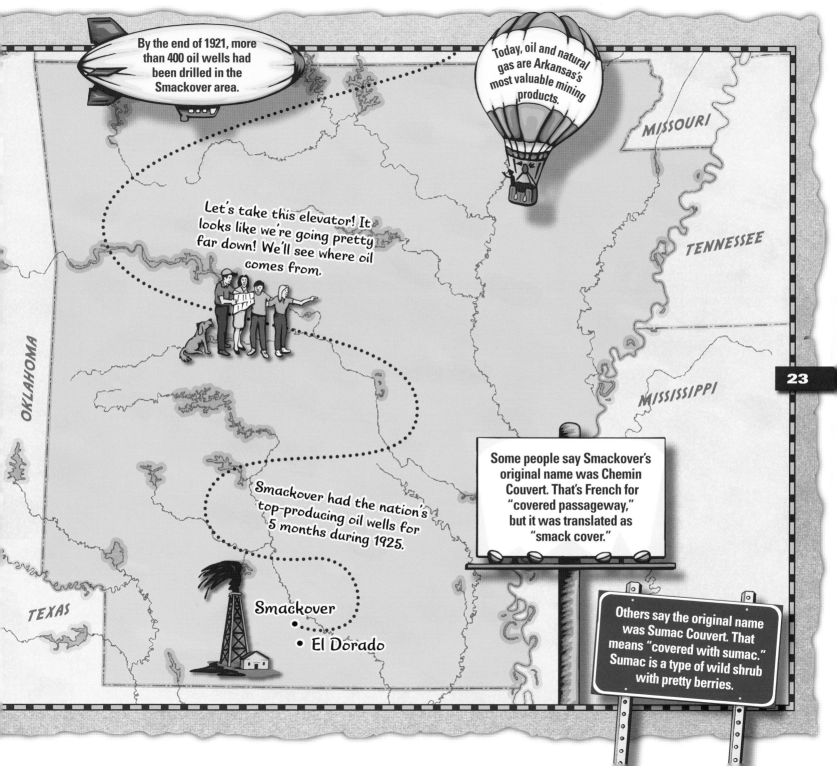

By the end of 1921, more than 400 oil wells had been drilled in the Smackover area.

Today, oil and natural gas are Arkansas's most valuable mining products.

MISSOURI

TENNESSEE

Let's take this elevator! It looks like we're going pretty far down! We'll see where oil comes from.

MISSISSIPPI

OKLAHOMA

Some people say Smackover's original name was Chemin Couvert. That's French for "covered passageway," but it was translated as "smack cover."

Smackover had the nation's top-producing oil wells for 5 months during 1925.

TEXAS

Smackover
• Smackover
• El Dorado

Others say the original name was Sumac Couvert. That means "covered with sumac." Sumac is a type of wild shrub with pretty berries.

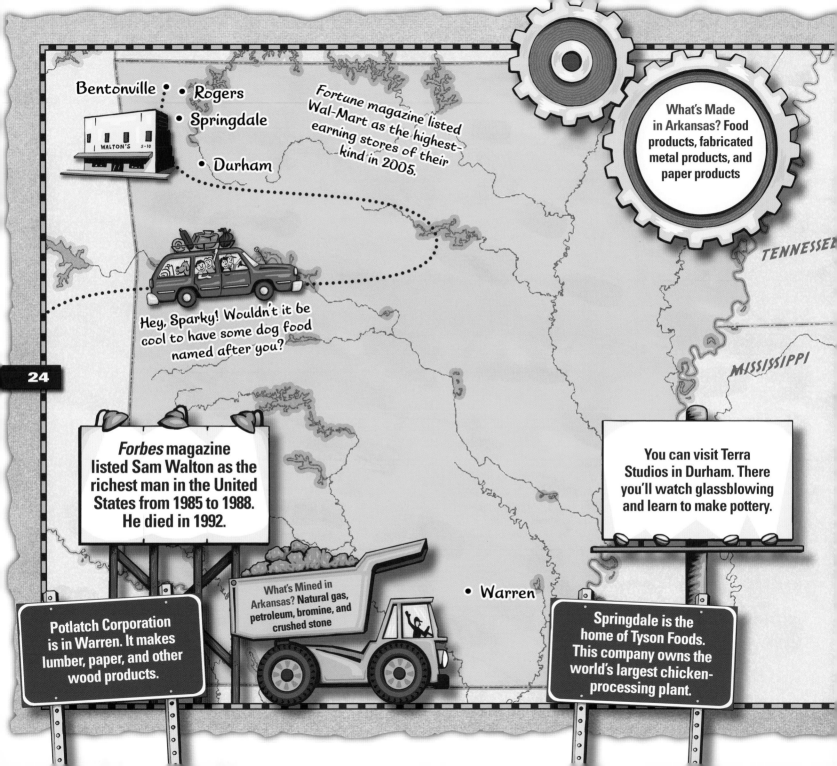

Bentonville • • Rogers

• Springdale

WALTON'S 5-10

• Durham

Fortune magazine listed Wal-Mart as the highest-earning stores of their kind in 2005.

What's Made in Arkansas? Food products, fabricated metal products, and paper products

TENNESSEE

MISSISSIPPI

Hey, Sparky! Wouldn't it be cool to have some dog food named after you?

Forbes magazine listed Sam Walton as the richest man in the United States from 1985 to 1988. He died in 1992.

You can visit Terra Studios in Durham. There you'll watch glassblowing and learn to make pottery.

What's Mined in Arkansas? Natural gas, petroleum, bromine, and crushed stone

• Warren

Potlatch Corporation is in Warren. It makes lumber, paper, and other wood products.

Springdale is the home of Tyson Foods. This company owns the world's largest chicken-processing plant.

Wal-Mart's Birthplace in Bentonville

Have you ever been to Wal-Mart? These stores are named after Sam Walton. In 1950, he opened a little store in Bentonville. Now there are Wal-Mart stores all over the world!

You can visit Walton's first Bentonville store. It's called the Wal-Mart Visitor's Center now. It's like a museum of Wal-Mart history. You'll see Sam's old office and pickup truck. And you'll see some Ol' Roy Dog Food. It was named after Sam's dog!

Stores such as Wal-Mart are busy in Arkansas. So are factories. Food products are the state's major factory goods. Many factories make paper and metal goods, too.

Stop by the Wal-Mart Visitor's Center. It's more than your average grocery store!

The 1st store with the name Wal-Mart opened in Rogers in 1962.

Wal-Mart has more than 5,200 stores. Most are in the United States.

Would you make a good scientist? Head to the Arkansas Museum of Discovery and find out!

The Arkansas River Visitor Center is in Russellville. It shows how the Arkansas River Navigation System works.

Little Rock's Arkansas Museum of Discovery

Use your body's energy to turn lights on. Feel electricity making your hair stand straight out. Meet creepy, crawly bugs and even hold some. See what the dentist sees inside your mouth. You're exploring the Arkansas Museum of Discovery!

Scientific discoveries helped Arkansas grow. Scientists and engineers developed better farm equipment. Farms then needed fewer workers. People moved to cities for factory work.

Waterway engineers improved the Arkansas River, too. Then large chains of **barges** could use the river. This brought new business to Arkansas's river ports. Look for barges when you cross the Arkansas River!

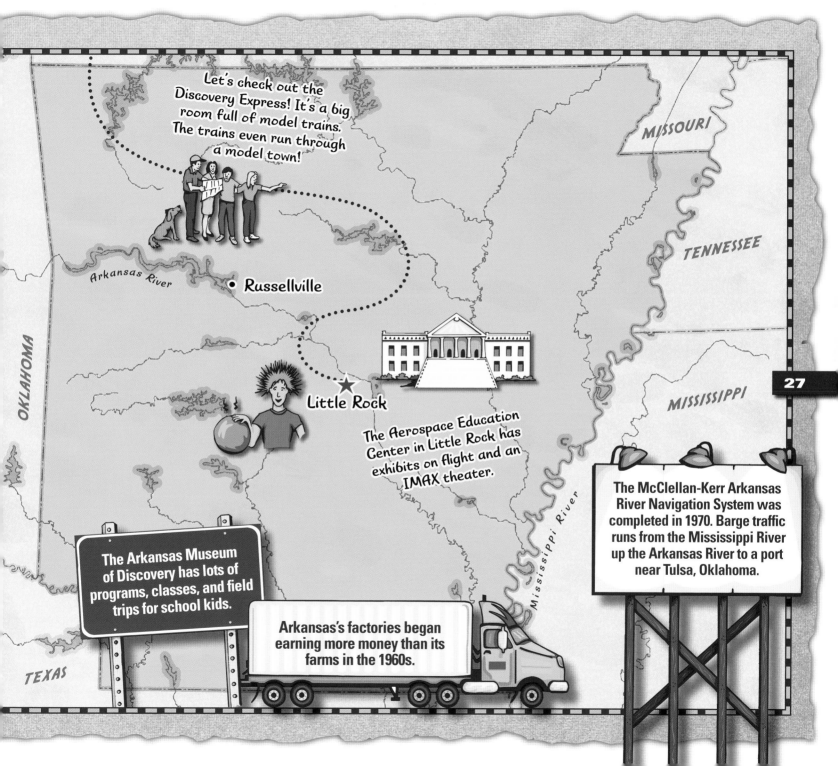

Let's check out the Discovery Express! It's a big room full of model trains. The trains even run through a model town!

MISSOURI

TENNESSEE

Arkansas River

● Russellville

★ Little Rock

MISSISSIPPI

The Aerospace Education Center in Little Rock has exhibits on flight and an IMAX theater.

The McClellan-Kerr Arkansas River Navigation System was completed in 1970. Barge traffic runs from the Mississippi River up the Arkansas River to a port near Tulsa, Oklahoma.

OKLAHOMA

Mississippi River

The Arkansas Museum of Discovery has lots of programs, classes, and field trips for school kids.

Arkansas's factories began earning more money than its farms in the 1960s.

TEXAS

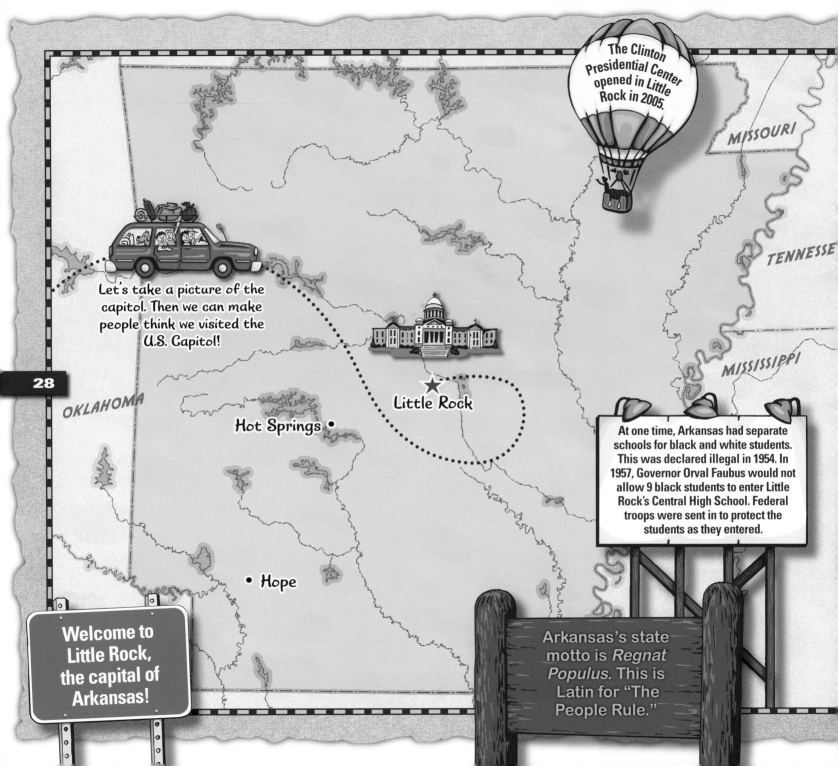

The Clinton Presidential Center opened in Little Rock in 2005.

MISSOURI

TENNESSEE

MISSISSIPPI

Let's take a picture of the capitol. Then we can make people think we visited the U.S. Capitol!

OKLAHOMA

Little Rock

Hot Springs

• Hope

At one time, Arkansas had separate schools for black and white students. This was declared illegal in 1954. In 1957, Governor Orval Faubus would not allow 9 black students to enter Little Rock's Central High School. Federal troops were sent in to protect the students as they entered.

Welcome to Little Rock, the capital of Arkansas!

Arkansas's state motto is *Regnat Populus.* This is Latin for "The People Rule."

The State Capitol in Little Rock

The Old State House in Little Rock was the 1st state capitol. Now it houses a museum of Arkansas history.

Does the capitol look familiar to you? It should. It looks like the U.S. Capitol in Washington, D.C. That's where the nation's lawmakers meet. Sometimes moviemakers want to show the U.S. Captiol. They film the Arkansas capitol instead!

Many state government offices are in the capitol. Arkansas's state government has three branches. One branch makes the laws. Its members belong to the General Assembly. They meet in the capitol. A second branch carries out the laws. It's headed by the governor. Judges make up the third branch of government. They decide whether someone has broken the law.

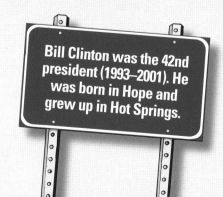

Is that the U.S. Capitol? No, it's Arkansas's capitol in Little Rock!

Bill Clinton was the 42nd president (1993–2001). He was born in Hope and grew up in Hot Springs.

Stuttgart is home to the Stuttgart Agricultural Museum. It shows how Arkansas became the nation's top rice producer.

An Arkansas farmer inspects his picked cotton crop.

Warren is in Bradley County. Farmers there grow pink tomatoes—Bradleys and Arkansas Travelers. Look for them in farmers' markets.

Warren's Pink Tomato Festival

Do you like tomatoes? Then try the tomato-eating contest. Are you a good artist? You might win the tomato-coloring contest. Are you still hungry? Then belly up to the all-tomato lunch. You're at the Pink Tomato Festival!

Tomatoes are a delicious Arkansas product. But rice and cotton are the leading crops. No other state grows more rice.

Arkansas is a top chicken state, too. Chickens bring in the most farm income. Many farmers raise beef cattle, hogs, and turkeys. Wild turkeys live in the woods. Want a turkey to come running? Then practice your turkey calls. Turkey calling is a fine art in Arkansas!

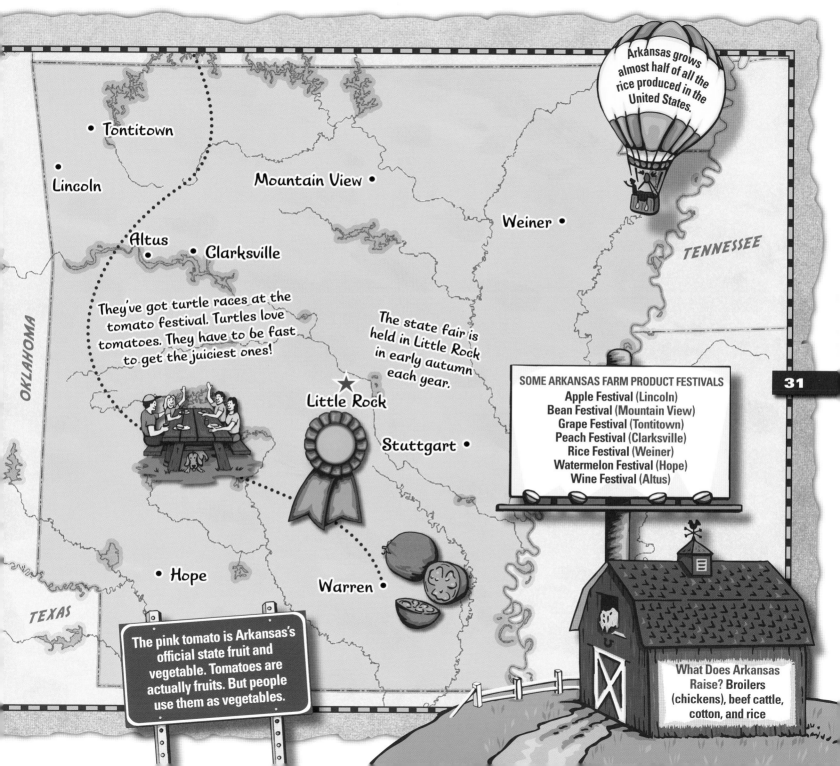

Arkansas grows almost half of all the rice produced in the United States.

• Tontitown

Mountain View •

• Lincoln

Weiner •

TENNESSEE

Altus • Clarksville

They've got turtle races at the tomato festival. Turtles love tomatoes. They have to be fast to get the juiciest ones!

The state fair is held in Little Rock in early autumn each year.

OKLAHOMA

★
Little Rock

Stuttgart •

SOME ARKANSAS FARM PRODUCT FESTIVALS
Apple Festival (Lincoln)
Bean Festival (Mountain View)
Grape Festival (Tontitown)
Peach Festival (Clarksville)
Rice Festival (Weiner)
Watermelon Festival (Hope)
Wine Festival (Altus)

• Hope

Warren •

TEXAS

The pink tomato is Arkansas's official state fruit and vegetable. Tomatoes are actually fruits. But people use them as vegetables.

What Does Arkansas Raise? Broilers (chickens), beef cattle, cotton, and rice

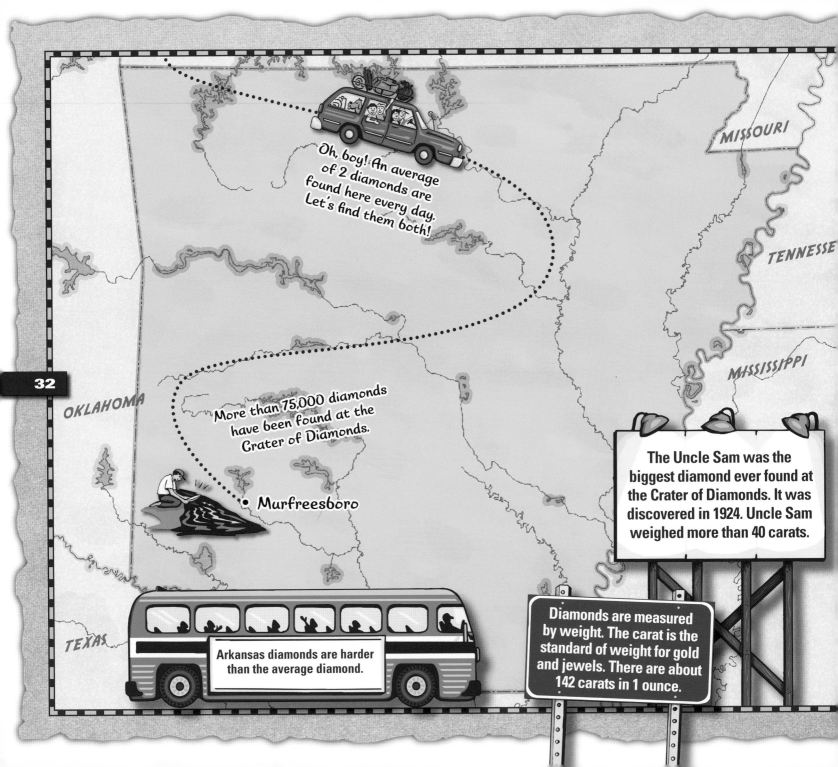

MISSOURI

TENNESSEE

MISSISSIPPI

OKLAHOMA

TEXAS

Oh, boy! An average of 2 diamonds are found here every day. Let's find them both!

More than 75,000 diamonds have been found at the Crater of Diamonds.

• Murfreesboro

The Uncle Sam was the biggest diamond ever found at the Crater of Diamonds. It was discovered in 1924. Uncle Sam weighed more than 40 carats.

Arkansas diamonds are harder than the average diamond.

Diamonds are measured by weight. The carat is the standard of weight for gold and jewels. There are about 142 carats in 1 ounce.

Bring your bucket and shovel. Then start digging for diamonds. What if you find one? Finders keepers!

You're diamond hunting at the Crater of Diamonds. It's the nation's only diamond-mining site. Thousands of diamonds have been found there. Most are tiny, but some are huge. And you're welcome to find some, too!

Diamonds aren't sparkly when you dig them up. They're sort of dark and greasy looking. How can you tell a diamond from gravel? Park workers help you. They teach you what raw diamonds look like. And they show you how to search. Good luck!

Keep your eyes peeled! You might find a diamond!

You might also find garnets, amethysts, jasper, agates, and quartz at the Crater of Diamonds.

33

Mastodons ate plants. Their tusks helped them gather food. They used their tusks for fighting, too.

Meet Mona the Mastodon

Watch out! She's pretty tall. In fact, you barely come up to her knees. She's Mona the mastodon!

Mastodons are relatives of elephants. They lived millions of years ago. They had shaggy coats and long, curved tusks. Mona is a copy of a real mastodon skeleton. You'll find her in Jonesboro. She's in the Arkansas State University Museum.

Arkansas was a great place for mastodons. They've been found in twenty sites there. Mastodons disappeared about 10,000 years ago. Now, take a long look at Mona. Are you glad or sad that mastodons are gone?

Nice to meet you, Mona! Giant mastodons once called Arkansas home.

Mastodons first lived in Africa. From there, they spread to Europe and Asia. They reached North America about 14 million years ago.

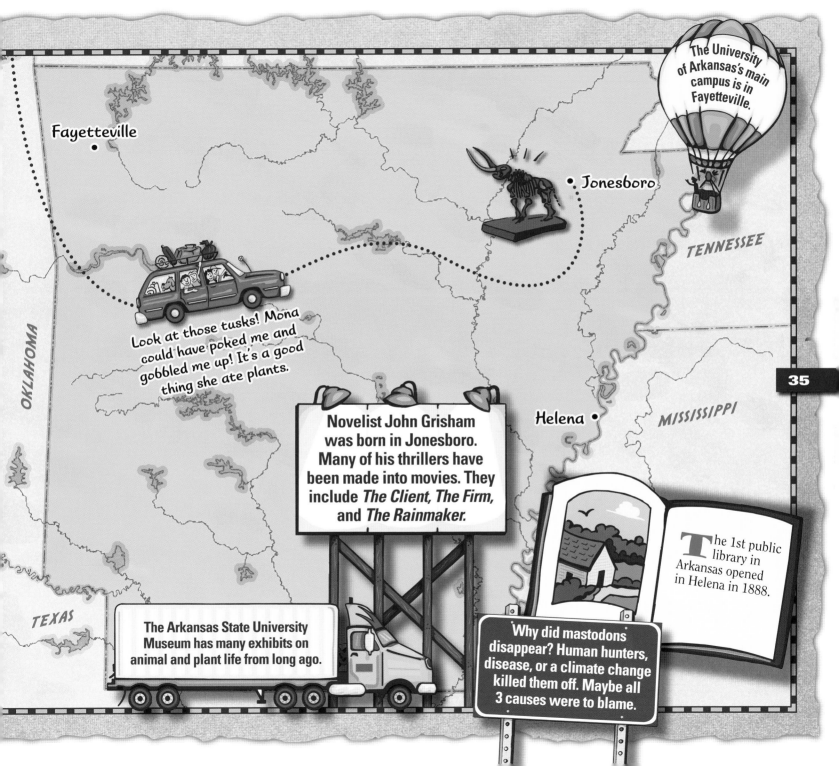

The University of Arkansas's main campus is in Fayetteville.

Fayetteville

Jonesboro

TENNESSEE

OKLAHOMA

Look at those tusks! Mona could have poked me and gobbled me up! It's a good thing she ate plants.

Helena

MISSISSIPPI

Novelist John Grisham was born in Jonesboro. Many of his thrillers have been made into movies. They include *The Client, The Firm,* and *The Rainmaker.*

The 1st public library in Arkansas opened in Helena in 1888.

TEXAS

The Arkansas State University Museum has many exhibits on animal and plant life from long ago.

Why did mastodons disappear? Human hunters, disease, or a climate change killed them off. Maybe all 3 causes were to blame.

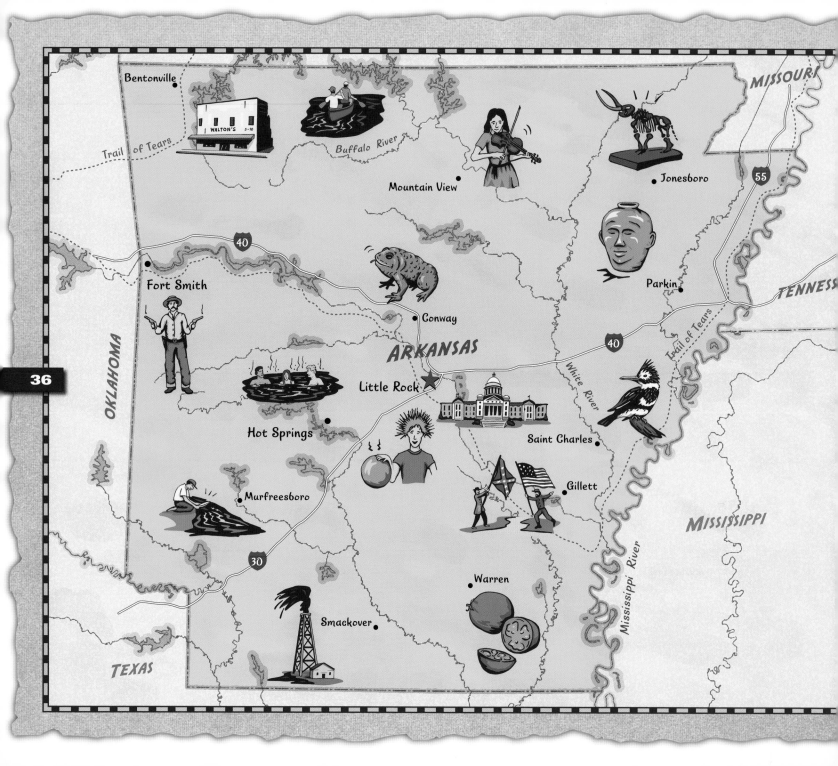

MISSOURI

Bentonville

Trail of Tears

WALTON'S 5-10

Buffalo River

Mountain View

Jonesboro

Parkin

TENNESSEE

40

Fort Smith

Conway

ARKANSAS

Little Rock

White River

40

Trail of Tears

55

OKLAHOMA

Hot Springs

Saint Charles

Murfreesboro

Gillett

MISSISSIPPI

30

Warren

Smackover

Mississippi River

TEXAS

OUR TRIP

We visited many amazing places on our trip! We also met a lot of interesting people along the way. Look at the map on the left. Use your fingers to trace all the places we have been.

What is the high and rugged section of the Ozarks called? See page 7 for the answer.

How many gallons of water come from Hot Springs each day? Page 8 has the answer.

What is the name of the University of Arkansas's mascot? See page 10 for the answer.

Which city holds the World-Famous Armadillo Festival? Look on page 12 for the answer.

When was Arkansas Post the capital of Arkansas Territory? Page 16 has the answer.

Where was country singer Johnny Cash born? Turn to page 19 for the answer.

How many stores does Wal-Mart have? Look on page 25 for the answer.

What is Arkansas's official state fruit and vegetable? Turn to page 31 for the answer.

That was a great trip! We have traveled all over Arkansas.
There are a few places that we didn't have time for, though. Next time, we plan to visit the Arkansas Alligator Farm and Petting Zoo in Hot Springs. They have over 300 alligators. Some are up to 12 feet (3.7m) long! Visitors can also see deer, goats, llamas, ostriches, and lambs.

More Places to Visit in Arkansas

WORDS TO KNOW

archeological (ar-kee-oh-LOJ-ik-uhl) relating to the study of remains left by early humans

barges (BAR-jez) long boats with flat bottoms

bathhouse (BATH-houss) a building where people take healthful baths

derricks (DER-iks) towers with equipment for drilling into the ground for oil

extinct (ek-STINGKT) no longer existing

gallows (GAL-ohz) structures used for hangings

historians (hi-STOR-ree-unz) people who study events in history

industry (IN-duh-stree) a type of business

pioneers (pye-uh-NEERZ) people who settle in a new area

Arkansas covers 52,068 square miles (134,856 sq km). It's the 27th-largest state in size.

STATE SYMBOLS

State beverage: Milk

State bird: Mockingbird

State flower: Apple blossom

State folk dance: Square dance

State fruit and vegetable: South Arkansas vine ripe pink tomato

State gem: Diamond

State insect: Honeybee

State mammal: White-tailed deer

State mineral: Quartz crystal

State musical instrument: Fiddle

State rock: Bauxite

State tree: Pine

State flag

State seal

STATE SONG

Besides the state anthem, Arkansas has 2 official state songs. They are "Arkansas (You Run Deep in Me)" by Wayland Holyfield and "Oh, Arkansas" by Terry Rose and Gary Klaff. Arkansas also has an official state historical song, "The Arkansas Traveler."

"Arkansas"
Words and music by Eva Ware Barnett

I am thinking tonight of the Southland,
Of the home of my childhood days,
Where I roamed through the woods and the meadows
By the mill and the brook that plays;
Where the roses are in bloom
And the sweet magnolia too,
Where the jasmine is white
And the fields are violet blue,
There a welcome awaits all her children
Who have wandered afar from home.

Chorus:
Arkansas, Arkansas, 'tis a name dear,
'Tis the place I call "home, sweet home";
Arkansas, Arkansas, I salute thee,
From thy shelter no more I'll roam.

'Tis a land full of joy and of sunshine,
Rich in pearls and in diamonds rare,
Full of hope, faith, and love for the stranger,
Who may pass 'neath her portals fair;
There the rice fields are full,
And the cotton, corn and hay,
There the fruits of the field,
Bloom in the winter months and May,
'Tis the land that I love, first of all, dear,
And to her let us all give cheer.

(Chorus)

FAMOUS PEOPLE

Angelou, Maya (1928–), author and poet

Bates, Daisy Lee Gatson (1914–1999), civil rights activist

Cash, Johnny (1932–2003), singer and songwriter

Cleaver, Eldridge (1935–1998), civil rights activist and author

Clinton, Bill (1946–), 42nd U.S. president

Dean, "Dizzy" (1910–1974), baseball player

Fletcher, John Gould (1886–1950), poet

Fulbright, J. William (1905–1995), politician and educator

Green, David Gordon (1975–), film director

Grisham, John (1955–), novelist

Joplin, Scott (1868–1917), composer and pianist

Ladd, Alan (1913–1964), actor

MacArthur, Douglas (1880–1964), World War II general

Martin, Mark (1959–), NASCAR driver

Pippen, Scottie (1965–), basketball player

Saracen (ca. 1735–1832), American Indian chief

Stone, Edward Durell (1902–1978), architect

Thornton, Billy Bob (1955–), actor

Walton, Sam (1918–1992), founder of Wal-Mart

Wood, Audrey (1930–), children's book author and illustrator

TO FIND OUT MORE

At the Library

Gaines, Ann. *William J. Clinton: Our Forty-Second President.* Chanhassen, Minn.: The Child's World, 2002.

Jones, Brenn. *Learning about Achievement from the Life of Maya Angelou.* New York: PowerKids Press, 2002.

Lucas, Eileen, and Mark Anthony (illustrator). *Cracking the Wall: The Struggles of the Little Rock Nine.* Minneapolis: Carolrhoda Books, 1997.

Peterson, Brian C. *Mark Martin: Perennial Contender.* Maple Plain, Minn.: Tradition Books, 2004.

Shoulders, Michael, and Rick Anderson (illustrator). *N Is for Natural State: An Arkansas Alphabet.* Chelsea, Mich.: Sleeping Bear Press, 2003.

On the Web

Visit our home page for lots of links about Arkansas: *http://www.childsworld.com/links*

Note to Parents, Teachers, and Librarians: We routinely verify our Web links to make sure they are safe, active sites—so encourage your readers to check them out!

Places to Visit or Contact

Arkansas Department of Parks and Tourism
One Capitol Mall
Little Rock, AR 72201
800/628-8725
For more information about traveling in Arkansas

Arkansas History Commission
One Capitol Mall
Little Rock, AR 72201
501/682-6900
For more information about the history of Arkansas

INDEX

Bye, Land of Opportunity. We had a great time. We'll come back soon!